This book belongs to

_____

Walt Disney ®

OUR
WONDERFUL EARTH

WALT DISNEY FUN-TO-LEARN LIBRARY

A BANTAM BOOK
TORONTO · NEW YORK · LONDON · SYDNEY · AUCKLAND

Our Wonderful Earth   A Bantam Book/January 1983   All rights reserved. Copyright © 1983 by Walt Disney Productions. This book may not be reproduced, in whole or in part, by mimeograph or any other means.

ISBN 0-553-05513-5

Published simultaneously in the United States and Canada. Bantam Books are published by Bantam Books, Inc. Its trademark, consisting of the words "Bantam Books" and the portrayal of a rooster, is Registered in U.S. Patent and Trademark Office and in other countries. Marca Registrada. Bantam Books, Inc., 666 Fifth Avenue, New York, New York 10103. Printed in the United States of America   0 9 8 7 6

Classic® binding, R. R. Donnelley & Sons Company. U.S. Patent No. 4,408,780; Patented in Canada 1984; Patents in other countries issued or pending.

Imagine that you are up in a spaceship. How do you think the place where you live will look? You won't be able to see the town you live in because it's too small. What you will see is most of Earth, all at once.

From your spaceship the earth you live on will look like a huge ball, turning slowly in space. And instead of trees or houses, you will see colors. The blue is the blue of the oceans. Brown patches are mountains. The green is the green of the forests. And all around Earth are white, swirling clouds.

When we're standing on Earth, we can't see that it's a ball. Down here, Earth seems flat, and we can only see a little bit of it at a time.

But Earth is full of wonderful things to see and wonderful places to explore. There are deserts, jungles, forests, and rivers. There are high mountains and deep, blue oceans. There are even places where it is winter, all year long. Come, join Mickey and his friends as they set out to discover our wonderful Earth.

Donald wants the boys to see what the world looks like from the top of a mountain. The trail up the mountain isn't too steep at first, and they see plenty of trees and wild flowers. But the higher they go, the steeper the trail becomes, and the fewer plants and trees they see.

"Come on, boys," says Donald, huffing and puffing.

The next part of the trail takes them over big rocks and patches of snow. It's so cold up here, the snow never goes away, not even in summer. But before they know it, they've made it to the top.

From the top of the mountain, the trees look like tiny green specks, and the towns look like toy villages.

"We can play king of the mountain," says Huey. "I claim those towns over there."

The boys found a little stream at the top of the mountain.
Let's join them to see where it goes.

The stream starts as a trickle of melting snow, running
downhill from the top of the mountain. Then it joins with other
streams and gets bigger and bigger.

Soon it flows faster and faster, rushing down the
mountainside.

Here it spills over a rocky ledge to make a waterfall.

Then the water moves more slowly. Still other rivers join to make it bigger.

At last it's a wide, deep river that Huey, Dewey, and Louie can float on with their raft.

And where do you suppose it goes?

It joins the ocean—the place where it was headed all along. Now that the boys are at the ocean, wouldn't it be a shame if they didn't go in for a swim? There goes Dewey, with a great big splash. He loves to swim in the ocean because the salt water makes it easier to float. And what could be more fun than riding the waves? Waves are giant ripples that rise up as the wind blows over the water.

Back on the beach Huey and Louie go hunting for shells. They find shiny shells with curly backs, ruffly scallop shells, and some that look like spinning tops.

"That used to be the home of a snail," says Louie.

"I'm glad we found the shells before the waves did," says Huey. "Some of this sand is made up of shells that the ocean broke up into tiny pieces."

What if Morty and Ferdie found a magic cave with stairs that went deep into Earth? First they'd walk down through layers of rock. Each layer would be below the other like the layers on a cake. The farther they went, the hotter it would get. Even the rocks would be melted, or molten. Look, Morty, the heat is making the rocks above crack and split!

Sometimes the great heat inside Earth makes the top
layers crack open. And up comes the melted rock, like a red-hot,
fiery fountain. We call this a volcano.

Soon Minnie and Goofy join Morty and Ferdie in their magic cave. The walls of the cave glitter with different-colored rocks and sparkling minerals.

Ferdie picks up a stone that looks like yellow glass. As it breaks up in his hand, he hears a crackling noise.

"That's what happens when a special kind of rock gets hot," explains Minnie. "This kind of rock has sulfur in it."

"Look what I've found." Morty holds up chunks of clear, boxlike crystals.

"Taste them," says Minnie.

"They're salty," cries Morty, surprised.

"That's where salt comes from," says Minnie.

Just then she finds a lump of glistening, purple crystals.

"Daisy has a ring that color," says Morty. "Isn't that called amethyst?"

"There's another one near your foot, Goofy," says Minnie.

"Aw, that's just a plain old rock."

But when he splits it open, "Gawrsh!" he says. "It's beautiful inside, just like yours!"

Do you like being outside on a windy day? On a windy afternoon, Mickey takes Morty and Ferdie out for a ride in their sailboat. As the wind blows Donald's balloon away, Morty asks, "I know our boat floats in water, but what is the balloon floating in?"

"It's floating in our ocean of air," replies Mickey. "There's a blanket of air all around Earth. We breathe air, birds fly in it, but we can't see it."

"Then how do we know it's really there?" asks Ferdie.

"What is spinning Goofy's pinwheel? What carried away Minnie's hat? The wind, of course. And do you know what wind is? Wind is nothing but moving air," explains Mickey.

When the wind is moving very fast, we can hear it whistle. It may even sting your face. So, you see, even though we can't see air, there are many ways to prove that it really *is* there!

Today, Mickey is taking Morty and Ferdie with their sailboat
to the beach. They want to explore Pirates' Island. But when
they get there, they can't even see the water.

"Being in a fog is like being in a cloud," says Morty.

"A very big, thick cloud," adds Ferdie.

"Yes," says Mickey. "In fact, on different kinds of days, you
will find that the clouds are different shapes and sizes, too."

When clouds are soft and puffy and high up in the sky, we have a mostly sunny day.

But sometimes clouds cover the sun so we can't see it. Then we have a cloudy day. When these clouds get very close to Earth, we know it's going to rain.

Sometimes tall, dark clouds tell us a storm is coming. We may even have thunder and lightning.

Did you know there are some places on Earth where it's hot or cold or rainy or sunny—all year long?

Mickey and Goofy are off on an extra special adventure. They are going to explore a part of Earth that is hot and rainy all year round.

They find a hot, steamy jungle, with huge trees and beautiful flowers. Monkeys swing in the trees and parrots squawk. Jaguars leap silently from branch to branch. Snakes slither through the long jungle grasses.

"I wish this rain would stop," says Goofy. "I'm getting wet!"

"Don't worry, Goofy, it will all be over in a few minutes, and the sun will dry us off."

It's a good thing Donald and Daisy brought their own water to drink. They're exploring the desert where it hardly ever rains. Just look at all that sand!

Donald and Daisy see a giant cactus with its thick, juicy stem that stores water. A cactus can wait a long time until it rains again.

Out here in the desert even the rocks are colorful and strange. Donald sees one that reminds him of Uncle Scrooge.

But there are animals here, too. Lizards and snakes like to lie in the sun. That's why the desert is a good home for them.

Some desert animals burrow underground or stay in shady places during the day. Then out they come at night to look for food.

Minnie is off on a special adventure with Morty and Ferdie.
They want to see what the coldest parts of Earth look like.
Here at the North Pole it seems like winter all year round.
Everything is covered with ice and snow. There are even rivers
of ice, called glaciers.

"That chunk of ice is as big as a ship!" cries Ferdie.
"That's an iceberg," says Minnie. "It looks like it's carrying some passengers, too."

Minnie and the boys come home from their North Pole adventure on the hottest day of the year. "The heat feels wonderful!" exclaim Morty and Ferdie, as they put on their bathing suits. "How lucky we are to have summer *and* winter where we live!"

Donald and Daisy are glad to be back home from the desert, even though at this very moment, they are getting a little wet. "I never thought I'd be glad to see rain," says Daisy. "But after all that sand..."

"Yes, it does feel good," agrees Donald. "I want to have fun with all these puddles while they last."

Mickey and Goofy come home from the jungle on a brisk, clear autumn day. "Isn't it funny that the leaves never change color in the jungle?" asks Goofy.

"Not really," replies Mickey. "There, it's hot and rainy all year round. Here, we have spring and summer and autumn and winter, so the trees and plants are always changing. Our garden really grew while we were away, Goofy!"

Huey, Dewey, and Louie love to explore Grandma Duck's farm. Each of the four seasons brings new ways to have fun there. In spring, everything seems new. Birds build their new nests. There are new baby animals. The trees grow new little leaves. Spring is when everything comes alive.

Spring rain makes great, muddy puddles. And with Huey around, they never go to waste.

In summer, the days are long and warm. Flowers bloom and ears of corn ripen in the cornfield. The leaves have grown big and fat on the trees. Huey, Dewey, and Louie sometimes go under them to cool off. Or sometimes, they go for a swim in the pond.

"Summer is a great time," says Louie.

In autumn, the days grow shorter. The boys help Grandma
Duck rake leaves—when they're not playing in them, that is.
Flowers and plants die, but seeds, fruits, and nuts have grown
where the flowers used to be. The boys don't mind at all. They
help with the harvest. And they love to pick apples for
Grandma's prize apple pies.

In winter, Grandma's farm is dark in the morning and dark in the evening. The trees have no leaves at all now, and the branches are covered with snow. Everything on the farm is resting. But if you look carefully, you will see buds on the branches. Inside the buds, new leaves are getting ready for spring.

Mickey, Morty, and Ferdie are watching the sunrise one morning from their mountain campsite. Little by little, they see the shapes around them more clearly.

"The sun is like Earth's very own light bulb," says Ferdie.

"You can't turn it off, though," says Mickey.

"Then how do we get night?" asks Ferdie.

Do you know the answer to Ferdie's question?
Remember when you where up in the spaceship and you
saw Earth turning? Night comes when the part of Earth you live on
turns away from the sun. When you're sleeping, it's daytime for
people on the other side of Earth. And when you wake up,
it's time for them to go to sleep!

Minnie, Morty, and Ferdie are watching shooting stars one night when Mortie says, "Look at the moon. Remember how the sun looked like a light bulb? Well, the moon looks like Earth's own night light!"

Nighttime is a good time to explore the sky, as Morty and Ferdie found. Did you ever notice how different the moon looks at different times of the month?

Sometimes, the moon looks thin — that's when the night looks darkest.

At other times, the moon looks bigger and rounder. That's when our nights are a little brighter, and we might not need a flashlight. And sometimes, we see the full moon, big and round and bright. Pluto thinks the "eyes" and "mouth" are real. But what looks like a face is only the shadows on the surface of the moon.

We've all seen the moon from down here, but what would it
be like to take a closer look?

If you landed on the moon, you would see deep craters and
dusty rocks. There are mountains here, too, but there are no
trees or plants to cover them. Nothing lives or grows on the
moon, not even the smallest animal or the tiniest plant.

There's no air on the moon, either. That's why astronauts
wear space suits and oxygen tanks. You might even find the
footprints of the astronauts who have landed there. There's no
wind on the moon, so those footprints will stay there forever.

Up here in space, the stars look very big and bright. But they don't sparkle because there is no air in space.

There are other bright lights in the sky. Those are the planets. They circle the sun along with our planet — Earth. Some are much bigger than Earth and some are smaller. One of them is called Pluto. Can you guess whose favorite planet that is?

Planets are huge balls in the sky. The ones you see here circle
our sun. But there are other suns in space and many other
planets we haven't seen yet — even from a spaceship. Do you
think there could be people living on them? Maybe one day,
we'll find out.

We're back! Are you glad to be home? A space trip is exciting, but if you look around you, you'll find so much more to discover — here on our wonderful Earth.